How to use this book

Whether we like it or not, devices are here to stay and are being used by children at younger and younger ages. This exposes them (and you) to increasing risks such as malware, viruses, exposure to pornography, cyber-grooming, identity theft, etc. **Empowering** children to navigate the cyber-world safely is what **My Device RULES!** is all about!

Even if your child is not yet using devices to connect to the internet, the earlier you teach them how to spot some of the risks and adopt healthy online habits, the more they will continue the practices throughout their life.

Although it is presented in a lighthearted way, **My Device RULES!** is designed around solid **principles of effective learning** so children can easily take away its very important message. How you deliver the book's content has an impact on the learning process, so here's some helpful advice to make your job easier.

Tip 1: **Make it fun and interactive!** Use the rhyme and vibrant drawings to engage your child. Really ask them the scenario questions, **let them think** before they answer, then move forward. Resist giving them the answers.

Tip 2: **Repetition** is one of the most important principles of early learning. Every time you come to **My Device RULES!** whether in full or in part, encourage your child to repeat each line after you. Work towards the point where they can say it at the same time as you and even better, **say it by themselves** (it's surprising how quickly they pick it up). When they can do that, you know they are well on the way to **My Device RULES!** being something they remember for life.

Tip 3: Similarly, read **My Device RULES!** with them regularly – once or twice a month. The more you read it together, the more its lessons will stay with your child.

Tip 4: Use the book to **create a conversation.** Technology and how it's used changes rapidly, so talk to your child about what they're doing. Your involvement and oversight is one of the most important ways you can assist their safety.

Tip 5: **Talk to others** about how you're using the book and how you're keeping your child digitally safe. Share tips between each other to gain inspiration. Visit our website www.mydevicerules.com for more ideas.

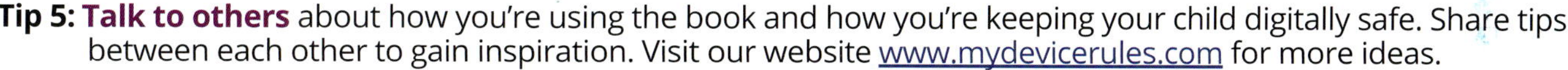

In addition, **take appropriate security precautions** on all technology your child accesses to give them the best chance of staying safe. There are many online recommendations on how to do that, so educate yourself and implement the best ones for your circumstances.

My Device RULES! is not a guarantee your child and their data will remain safe on their devices. But this book encourages kids to **think about what they're doing** and **education** is the first step towards empowerment. At the very least, you will forewarn your child of potential dangers without unnecessarily alarming them, and reinforce the importance of **speaking to someone they trust** should something happen or they're unsure. As parents ourselves, we hope your child navigates technology safely and discovers its power to assist their development.

Kate & Rod Power

Published by Kids Rule Publishing, Sydney Australia

For further enquiries, please visit:

Mydevicerules.com

Designed and set by Kids Rule Publishing

ISBN 978-0-9929530-4-1

Kids Rule Publishing

Kate & Rod Power

Click,
swirl,
scroll!

I'm on my game –

let's rock 'n roll!

Flick, tap, swipe...

Is that cat
playing bagpipes ?!?!

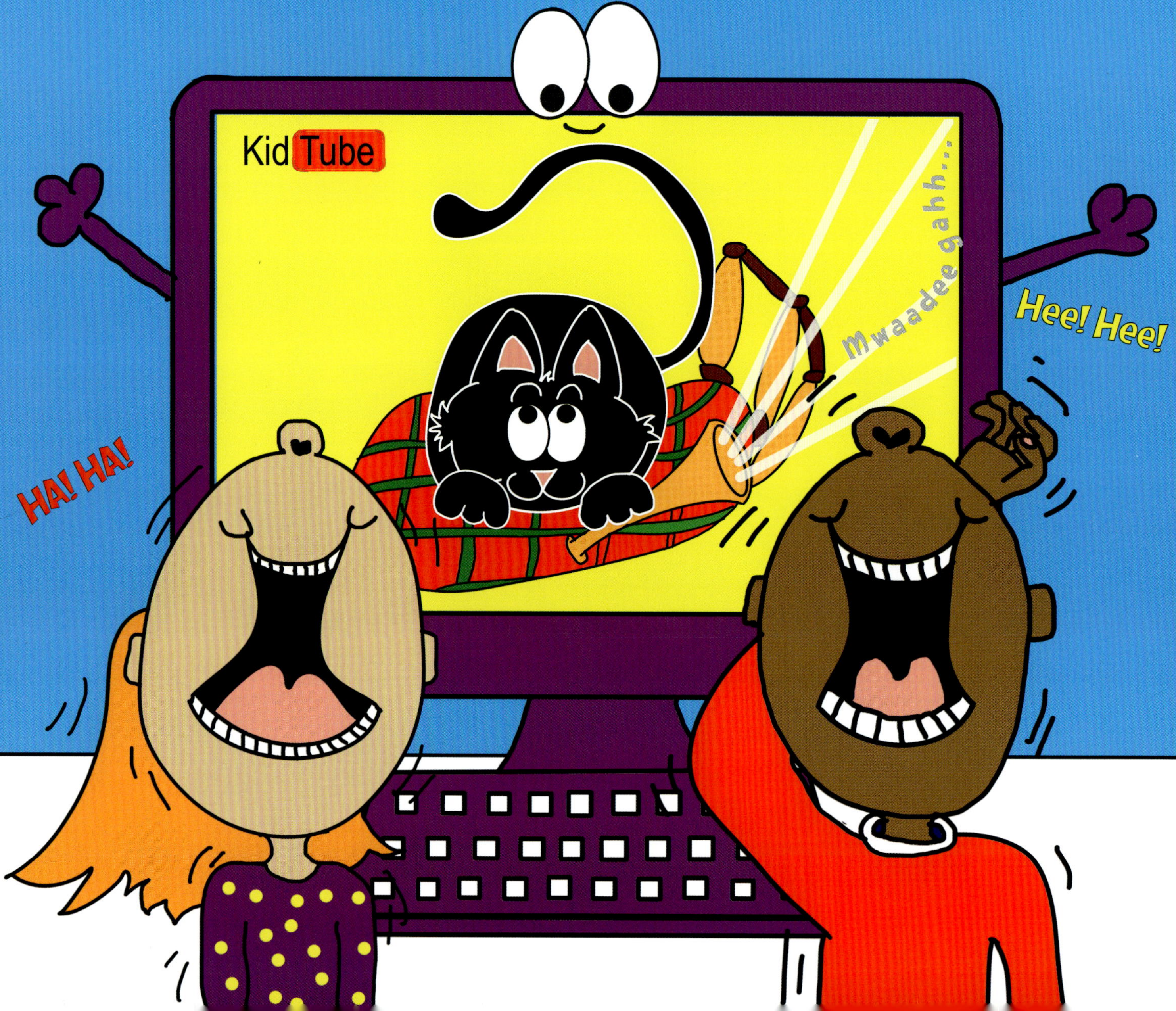

Kid Tube
Mwaadeegahh...
Hee! Hee!
HA! HA!

Devices are fun, devices are great
We can do, see and learn things -
even create!

But like other good stuff
We still must take care
You can swing on a swing...

too high in the air!

Or zoom
on a skateboard
straight into a chair!

Or bake
a nice cake but
singe all your hair!

Devices are nicest when we are aware
The things we see on them -
Vids, games, memes - the LOT
While sometimes are real, often they're NOT!

They're all made by people
Who aren't always kind
Some like to play tricks
And mess with our mind

But no need to worry
'Coz we're in control
If we keep to these rules
When we tap, swipe and scroll...

When I'm on my device
I have fun but think twice
'Coz I always take care what I do

If I see something weird
Or that makes me feel scared
I close it and hide it from view

I don't post my pic,
Name, age or address
Unless a safe grown-up says "Yes"

And if I'm on a shop
Or something pops up,
I ask what I can and can't press

Someone I don't know
Wants to chat I say "No"
'Coz I make my friends first in real life

And I say in this space
What I'd say to your face
That's how I keep my device nice!

Yes,
Devices are nice but they're only tools
That's why we always follow our rules.

Do you think you know them?
Let's see if it's true...
What would you do if this happened to you?

Question 1:

You're watching a vid or playing a game
And you see something icky,
too grown-up, or strange...

Just keep on going without any fuss
Or close it up quick
and tell someone you trust?

Close it up quick and tell someone you trust!

Who are your safe grown-ups?

When I'm on my device
I have fun but think twice
'Coz I always take care what I do

If I see something weird
Or that makes me feel scared
I close it and hide it from view

"Please enter your details"
blinks your device screen
With spaces to post things all blank,
bright and clean

What do you think -
fill it out straight away,
Or ask a safe grown-up
and see what they say?

Ask a safe grown-up and see what they say!
I don't post my pic, Name, age or address Unless a safe grown-up says yes!
It's best to keep our information safe!
Upload your photo
Give us your details

"Get this now, don't delay"
pops on your display
You just need to give it a click!
Will you be ok if you just press away,
Or should you ask if it's a trick?

Ask a safe grown-up if it's a trick!

Remember,
If I'm on a shop
Or something pops up,
I ask what I can and can't press

Question 4:

"Hey there, let's chat"
you suddenly see
But you're really unsure
who it might be...

Make a new friend
by sending back "Hi",
Or ignore them
no matter how hard they try?

Ignore them no matter how hard they try!

Someone I don't know
Wants to chat I say "No"
'Coz I make my friends first in real life

On devices, people can pretend to be someone they're not, so make friends in real life first!

Ask your friends what their device "names" are, so you know it's really them!

Question 5:

Your friend **WRITES** something
that makes you feel bad,
Perhaps it was hurtful
or just makes you mad...

Write back the first thing
that pops in your head,
Or wait 'til you've **thought**
it all through instead?

Wait 'til you've thought it all through!

You see,
Sometimes friends write and don't know how to say
What they want, and then it comes out the wrong way.
So why risk a friendship with words that are mean
You wrote from the safety of your device screen?

The last of our rules reminds what to do -
Keep your device nice...
and keep your friends too!

I say in this space
What I'd say to your face
That's how I keep my device nice!

AWESOME!!!
Great Answers!

Devices are fun, devices are great!
We can do, see and learn things –
even create
But you're even BETTER,
'coz they're only tools
And you keep yourself SAFE
with My Device RULES!

When I'm on my device
I have fun but think twice
'Coz I always take care what I do

If I see something weird
Or that makes me feel scared
I close it and hide it from view

I don't post my pic,
Name, age or address
Unless a safe grown-up says "Yes"

And if I'm on a shop
Or something pops up,
I ask what I can and can't press

Someone I don't know
Wants to chat I say "No"
'Coz I make my friends
first in real life

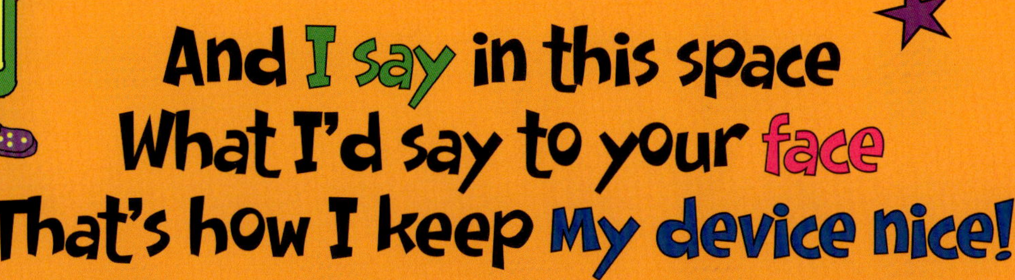

And I say in this space
What I'd say to your face
That's how I keep my device nice!

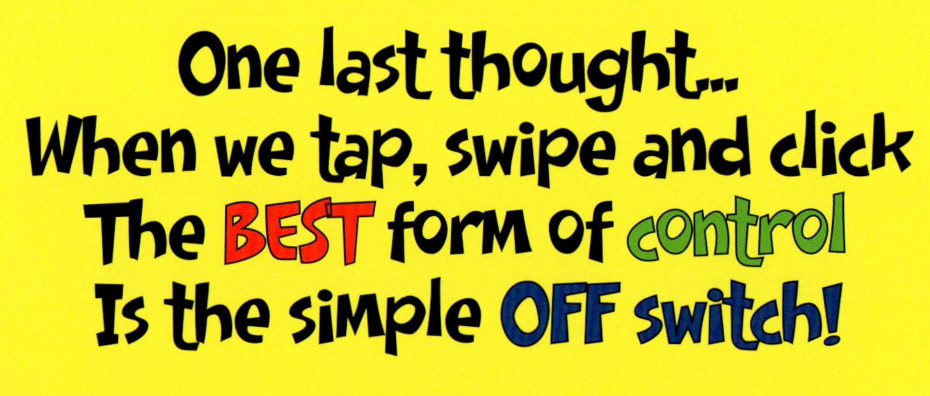

One last thought...
When we tap, swipe and click
The BEST form of control
Is the simple OFF switch!